Jean M. Thomsen Memorial Library
P.C
Ste
715-678-2872
W9-CCN-301

THOMAS & FRIENDS™
TALE of the BRAVE

Illustrated by Tommy Stubbs

A GOLDEN BOOK · NEW YORK

Thomas the Tank Engine & Friends™

CREATED BY BRITT ALLCROFT

Based on The Railway Series by The Reverend W Awdry.
© 2014 Gullane (Thomas) LLC.
Thomas the Tank Engine & Friends & Thomas & Friends are trademarks of Gullane (Thomas) Limited.
HIT and the HIT Entertainment logo are trademarks of HIT Entertainment Limited.
All rights reserved. Published in the United States by Golden Books, an imprint of Random House Children's Books, a division of Random House LLC, 1745 Broadway, New York, NY 10019, and in Canada by Random House of Canada Limited, Toronto, Penguin Random House Companies. Golden Books, A Golden Book, A Big Golden Book, the G colophon, and the distinctive gold spine are registered trademarks of Random House LLC.
randomhouse.com/kids   www.thomasandfriends.com
ISBN 978-0-385-37915-1
Printed in the United States of America
10 9 8 7 6 5 4 3 2
Random House Children's Books supports the First Amendment and celebrates the right to read.

JEAN M. THOMSEN
MEMORIAL LIBRARY
105 N. Gershwin Street
Stetsonville, WI 54480

It was a busy and bustling day at the clay pits on the Island of Sodor. Thomas was there helping out while a bridge on his Branch Line was being repaired. He liked working at the pits, but those troublesome engines, Bill and Ben, kept playing tricks on him.

There was no time for tricks that day, though. A friendly engine named Timothy warned everybody that rain might be coming. "And if it starts to rain, these clay walls will get really unstable. We'd best be careful today."

That afternoon, dark clouds filled the sky and cold rain started to fall. As Thomas cautiously rolled down some slippery tracks, the clay wall next to him began to drip and ooze. To his surprise, he saw strange marks under the sliding mud. They looked like giant footprints!

"But what kind of animal has feet that big?" Thomas wondered.

"Watch out!" Ben and Bill shouted. Before Thomas could get a good look at the footprints, the troublesome engines pushed him safely out of the way of a giant, gooey landslide.

The next morning, Sir Topham Hatt addressed the engines at the shunting yards. "Bill and Ben are best known for playing tricks on other engines. But by rescuing Thomas from yesterday's landslide, they have proven that they are Really Useful Engines!"

All the engines peeped happily, then rolled off to work. But Thomas couldn't stop thinking about the footprints.

Thomas returned to the clay pits, but he couldn't see the footprints. The tracks were closed and covered with mud.

Later, at Brendam Docks, Thomas told Percy about the footprints. "I don't know what could have made them. They were bigger than any animal on Sodor."

"Do you mean they are from a . . . monster?" Percy wheeshed.

"Don't be silly, Percy. There's no such thing as monsters."

For the rest of the day, Percy couldn't stop thinking about monsters. He didn't want to see anything scary. But later, as he came to the top of a hill, he did see a strange shape in the distance.

"What's that?" Percy puffed. "I hope it's not . . . a MONSTER!"

Percy reversed and raced backward all the way to the docks.

"It's the monster from the clay pits!" Percy whistled as he barreled into the docks. Everyone watched as something rumbled down the rails.

"That be no monster," Salty puffed. "That be an engine."

"I don't usually get mistaken for a monster," the big engine tooted. "Mind you, they do call me Gator. It seems they think my long water tanks make me look like an alligator."

Percy felt very silly for thinking the new engine was a monster.

Everywhere Percy went that night, he thought he saw strange creatures. Old trees and haystacks became monsters with clutching claws. Fluttering laundry on a clothesline looked like ghosts. Percy was so scared, he didn't even deliver the mail. He asked Thomas to pull the mail trucks. Thomas agreed to do it for one night.

The next morning, Thomas heard that the bridge on his Branch Line was open again. He was happy to go back to his usual work.

But James was unhappy. Sir Topham Hatt had asked him to pick up a load of scrap metal. "It's not fair," James puffed. "Thomas gets to pull coaches, and a fine engine like myself is sent to haul junk."

As James rolled off in a grumpy mood, he saw Percy. "Hello, scaredy-engine," he puffed. "Seen any monsters lately?"

"You can tease if you want," Percy peeped. "But Thomas saw giant footprints at the pits. There might be monsters on Sodor."

"Puff and nonsense!" James remarked as he rolled to the scrap yard.

James was busy thinking about monsters when he turned the corner into the scrap yard—and came face to face with jagged teeth and crooked claws!

"No!" James peeped. "Help!"

"Hello, mate," Reg the Scrap Crane puffed. "Looks like that scrap gave you a fright."

James realized it was only a pile of old gears and broken metal in front of him. "I'm not afraid of some broken old machines," he puffed.

Down at the docks, Percy was pleasantly surprised to find Gator waiting in a siding. "What are you doing here?" Percy asked.

"I'm heading to a new job," Gator puffed. "Unfortunately, my ship has been delayed. I have to wait until a new one can be found."

"At least you don't have to worry about sea monsters," Percy peeped.

"For all I know, sea monsters would be worried about *me*," Gator puffed with a laugh.

"Wow," Percy peeped. "I wish I were as brave as you."

"Being brave is not the same as not feeling scared, Percy. Being brave is what you do even when you feel scared. You might be braver than you think."

Inspired by Gator's words, Percy decided to be brave and pull the mail trucks all by himself that night. His boiler bubbled boldly as he chugged across the countryside. Nothing scared him—not the fluttering laundry, not the old, gnarled trees.

"Gator is right," he tooted. "I *can* be brave!"

Grumpy James was not nearly as happy. He needed to haul the Flying Kipper, which was full of fresh fish. As he rounded a bend in the woods, he saw a large, shadowy shape. He didn't realize it was only Gator.

His whistle screaming, James raced away. He was so frightened that he missed a red signal and jumped off the rails into a pond!

James was very embarrassed that Rocky had to hoist him out of the pond. When the other engines saw him at Knapford Junction, they had a good laugh.

"You were meant to *deliver* the fish," Henry puffed, "not throw them back in the water!"

James didn't like these jokes one bit. He'd show everyone that Percy was the real scaredy-engine, not him.

   That night, as Percy was delivering the mail, he saw
something unusual on the tracks—something big. This
definitely wasn't a haystack or a funny-looking engine.
It groaned and flashed its big teeth in the moonlight.
   Percy didn't want to be brave anymore. He dropped his
mail trucks and raced back to the sheds as fast as his little
wheels would carry him.

"The monster!" Percy whistled as he rolled to the sheds. "I really saw it!"

None of the other engines believed him. "You probably saw another haystack," James mocked.

Percy looked desperately to Thomas. "Tell them there really are monsters on Sodor. Tell them about the footprints you saw."

"I don't know what I saw," Thomas peeped. "But I don't think it was a monster."

"There's no such thing as monsters," steamed Henry. "Never was and never will be."

"Admit it, Percy, you're just a scaredy-engine," James peeped.

"But, James, you got a fright when you saw Gator!" Percy puffed.

"No, I didn't," James steamed. "I just missed a signal in the dark." He looked at the other engines. "I wasn't scared . . . like Percy!"

Early the next morning, Percy steamed away from the sheds to find his mail trucks. On the way, he saw Gator and asked him to come along. "You'll know what to do if we see any monsters."

"Monsters?" Gator puffed with a laugh. "You are a funny little engine."

"Well, it's good to have a new friend on the island," Percy peeped. "I'm glad you're not going away."

"But I am. My ship is here. I leave tonight."

Percy couldn't believe it.

Later that morning, Thomas saw James with a truckful of scrap. It was at the turn where Percy had seen the monster!

"James!" Thomas tooted. "You made a monster out of scrap metal to give Percy a fright."

"It was only a little joke," James replied.

"Not to Percy! You need to find him and tell him what you did . . . and apologize."

The two engines split up to find Percy.

Thomas found Percy at Knapford Station. He tried to tell him about James' prank, but Percy wouldn't listen.

"I thought you were my friend," Percy peeped. "When you told me about the footprints, I believed you. And when I told you about the monster, you should have believed me! Maybe I should go far away, like Gator!"

Percy puffed off in a huff.

Percy raced down to the docks and told Cranky to hoist him onto Gator's ship. "Are you sure Sir Topham Hatt wants you on this ship?" the big crane asked.

"Yes," Percy peeped. "I'm going to work far away, like Gator."

Percy was loaded onto the deck of the ship. It wasn't long before Gator was lowered next to him.

"I'm going to work in a faraway land," Percy puffed. "I'll show everyone how brave I can be!"

Gator thought for a moment. "But running away from your problems is not very brave, Percy."

Thomas chugged across Sodor looking for Percy. But when he heard a distant ship blow its horn, a terrible thought flew into his funnel.

"Oh, no!" Thomas peeped. "I know where Percy is going!"

Gator's ship was just leaving when Thomas reached the docks. "Cranky!" he whistled. "You have to stop that ship! It's an emergency!"

Cranky swung his hook and caught the ship's rail. His heavy chain rattled and strained as the great boat tried to pull away. The force was too great for Cranky. He started to tip over!

CREEEEAK!
Workmen on the ship tried to knock the hook loose with sledgehammers. Luckily, the captain was able to stop the ship before Cranky was pulled off the docks.

"Percy, come down!" Thomas whistled. "You can't leave! I'm sorry I didn't believe you!"

Gator peered over the railing of the ship. "Percy's not here."

"Percy?" Cranky groaned. "I unloaded him half an hour ago!"

Thomas could think of only one other place where Percy might go.

Night was falling as Percy quietly rolled through the clay pits. He stopped when he reached the warning signs. "If I can find the footprints, it will prove the monster is real," he thought. "Then everyone will know how brave I am."

At that moment, James rolled up. He started to apologize, but Percy interrupted him. "I'm braver than you'll ever be," Percy puffed.

James didn't like Percy's attitude. "If you're so brave, why have you stopped at the danger signs?"

"Being brave doesn't mean not being careful," Percy peeped.

"That's just what I thought a scaredy-engine would say!" puffed James as he pushed past Percy and the signs. He rolled into the narrow gorge. The cliff walls were still drippy and loose from the landslide.

"Oh, *monster*!" James called. "Come out, come out, wherever you are!"

Suddenly, James saw something in the moonlight. It had claws and teeth. "The monster!" wheeshed James. He tried to back up, but the walls began to rumble and tumble.

"It's another landslide!" Percy peeped. "You have to go forward, James!" The little green engine raced ahead to push James out of the way. Rocks hit Percy, and mud slid into his cab. And the big monster landed right in front of him!

That was when Percy made a discovery: it wasn't a monster. It was some sort of a rock!

The next day, Percy went to the Steamworks for a good cleaning. He had lots of mud in his funnel and gears. While he was there, James and Thomas visited and apologized.

"I hope we're still friends," Thomas peeped.

"Of course we are!" Percy replied. "We *all* are!"

All three engines wheeshed and whistled with joy.

That afternoon, Thomas carried a group of scientists to the clay pits. They were amazed by what Percy had found in the mud.

"It's a dinosaur fossil," one scientist explained to Thomas. "Fossils are what we call bones that have been in the ground for millions of years."

"So the monster was really a dinosaur from a long, long time ago," Thomas peeped in amazement. He couldn't wait to tell Percy.

Soon, the fossils were put on display in the Knapford Town Square. Excited families and curious engines came from all over the Island of Sodor to see them.

"A perfect specimen of a Megalosaurus!" the Earl of Sodor exclaimed. "How marvelous!"

Sir Topham Hatt addressed the crowd. "Today was made possible by a very special engine. Percy is not only a Really Useful Fossil Hunter but also one of the bravest engines on Sodor!"

The people clapped and cheered, and the engines blew their whistles . . . but Percy was nowhere to be seen.

Percy was at Brendam Docks, saying goodbye to Gator. Gator's ship was ready to depart again. As it steamed into the distance, Thomas and James pulled up alongside Percy.

"I guess you have to be brave to say goodbye to someone, too," Percy peeped.

"Did Gator say that?" Thomas asked.

"No, but he did say something else wise," Percy puffed, and his two friends rolled in closer to hear. "He said not to let James near any ponds or fish again."

Even James thought that was a funny joke. The three friends giggled and whistled with joy.

In the early 1940s, a loving father crafted a small blue wooden engine for his son, Christopher. The stories that this father, the Reverend W Awdry, made up to accompany the wonderful toy were first published in 1945. Reverend Awdry continued to create new adventures and characters until 1972, when he retired from writing.

Tommy Stubbs has been an illustrator for several decades. Lately, he has been illustrating the newest tales of Thomas and his engine friends, including *Hero of the Rails, Misty Island Rescue, Day of the Diesels,* and *King of the Railway.*